To my husband for his endless support, encouragement, and unconditional love.
To Billy and Gracie for allowing me to experience the greatest adventure of my life—being their mom.

www.mascotbooks.com

Billy & Gracie Unplugged Adventures: The Pirate Ship

©2019 Christina Trudden. All Rights Reserved. No part of this publication may be reproduced, stored in a retrieval system or transmitted in any form by any means electronic, mechanical, or photocopying, recording or otherwise without the permission of the author.

For more information, please contact:
Mascot Books
620 Herndon Parkway, Suite 320
Herndon, VA 20170
info@mascotbooks.com

Library of Congress Control Number: 2018909961

CPSIA Code: PRT1118A
ISBN-13: 978-1-64307-045-2

Printed in the United States

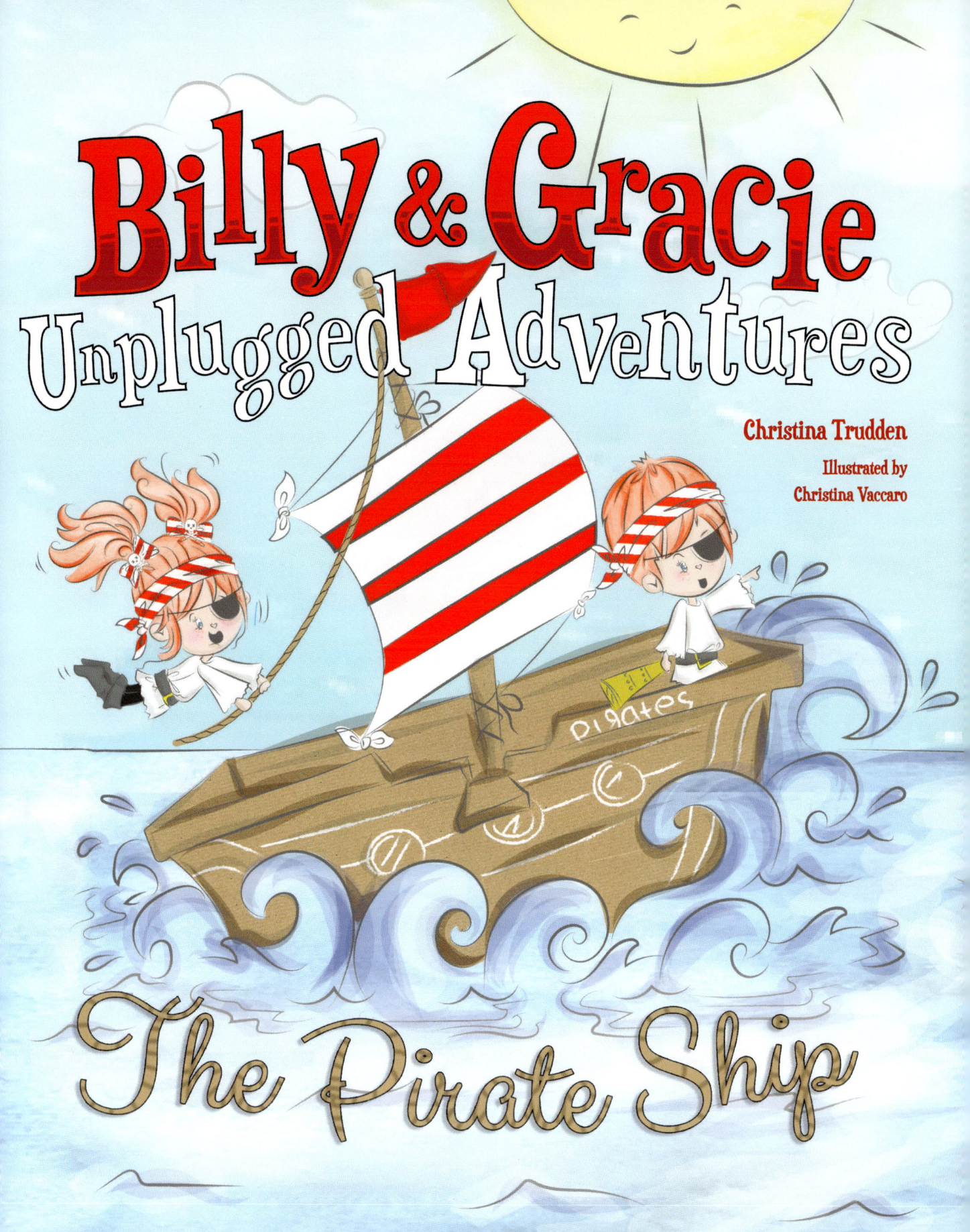

…live a set of twins with blueberry eyes, strawberry hair, and freckles the shape of hearts. Their names were **Billy and Gracie.**

One particular day while Billy and Gracie were binge watching their favorite TV show...

…their mother came in shouting, "Oh, no no no! That's enough, I can't take it anymore!"

She turned off the TV. "Not another minute, or I'll throw it out the door!"

Billy and Gracie cried and said, "But what are we to do?!"

Their mother just smiled. "Don't worry, it will come to you."

She then handed them a big cardboard box. In it were:

- Two pieces of black construction paper
- Two pieces of string
- A roll of tape
- A pair of scissors
- A box of crayons

"What are we supposed to do with this?" they said. But their mother had already left the room.

So they sat and thought and sat some more. All of this sitting and thinking made them realize they should open the front door.

When they did, what a sight it was! They had forgotten about the round green hill, the blooming pink flowers, the chirping bluebirds, the wooden swing in the tree...

...and the sunshine that warmed their faces.

Suddenly they were pirates on an adventure in a new and foreign land! They staked out their territory and began to understand what they could do with their box of supplies.

First, they got right to work making patches for their eyes.

Next, they turned their box into a pirate ship, and the lawn into the open sea.

Before they knew it, they were storming a beautiful castle.

Everywhere they looked, there was treasure to be found. Even rocks became glittering gold, all over the ground.

The more they imagined, the more riches they discovered.

Billy and Gracie ran into the house as fast as they could.

They were so excited to tell their parents about the day they had on the high seas and to eat dinner—of course! They were having so much fun they forgot to eat lunch!

Goodnight, Billy and Gracie. We are so proud that you found the adventure within you today. Our hope is that you find this excitement in everything you do, wherever you are. Even if all you need is a cardboard box. Always remember, your imagination will bring you anywhere you dare to go.

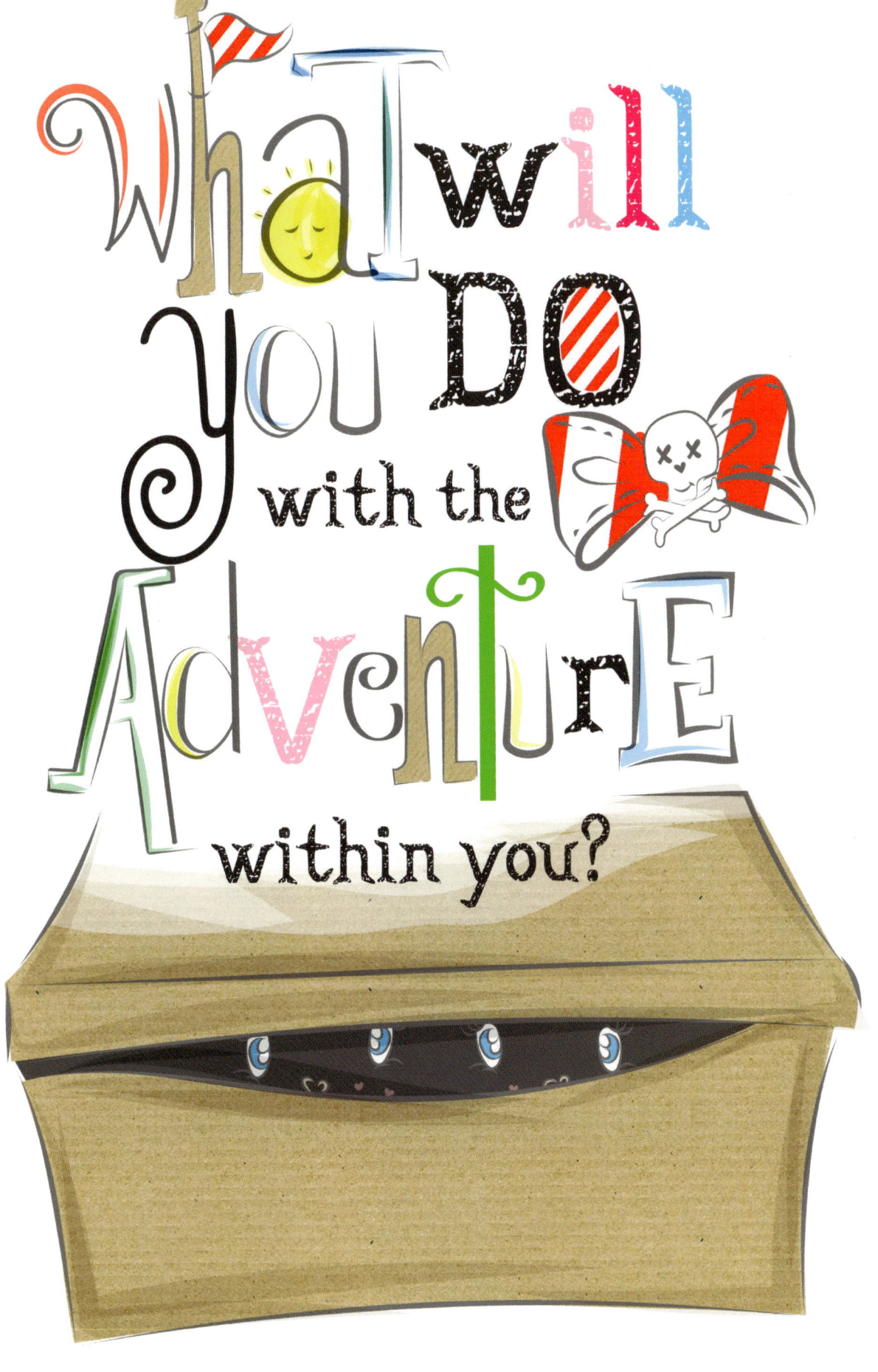

The End

About the Author

Christina received a BA in English from Quinnipiac University. After college, she worked as an advertising copywriter in New York City for 10 years. When her twins were born, she left advertising to raise them, and that's when she was inspired to write children's books. Christina always loved to read. As a young girl you would always find her curled up with a book, and to this day you still will. She is deeply passionate about instilling the love of literature in her own children. Christina resides on Long Island with the love of her life—her husband Bill—and their awesome twins Billy and Gracie.